For children everywhere, whose voices go unheard.

Illustrations copyright © 1998 by Debi Gliori
First published in Great Britain in 1998 by Bloomsbury Publishing Plc as
Give Him My Heart
First published in the United States by Holiday House, Inc. in 1998

Library of Congress Cataloging-in-Publication Data
Gliori, Debi.
What can I give him? / Debi Gliori.
p.   cm.
"Based on a poem by Christina Rossetti."
Summary: Two girls' stories entwine at Christmas as each must choose
a special gift for someone very important.
ISBN 0-8234-1392-6
1. Jesus Christ—Nativity—Juvenile Fiction.   [1. Jesus Christ—Nativity—Fiction.
2. Christmas—Fiction.   3. Gifts—Fiction.   4. Stories in rhyme.]
I. Rossetti, Christina Georgina, 1830–1894. II.Title.
PZ8.3.G47Wh 1998
[E]—dc21   98-11605
CIP
AC

WHAT CAN I GIVE HIM?

DEBI GLIORI

BASED ON A POEM BY CHRISTINA ROSSETTI

HOLIDAY HOUSE ♥ NEW YORK

In the bleak
midwinter

Frosty wind made moan

Earth stood hard
as iron

Water like a stone

Snow had fallen, snow on snow

Snow on snow

In the bleak midwinter
long, long ago

What can I give Him poor as I am

If I were a
shepherd
I would bring
a lamb

If I were a wise man
I would do my part

What I can I give Him

to Grandpa
with love

Give Him my heart

Christina Rossetti (1830–1894) was one of the
great nineteenth-century English poets. Her enduring legacy
includes *Goblin Market and Other Poems* and "A Christmas Carol,"
the poem in this book. "A Christmas Carol" is presented here
under the title "What Can I Give Him?"